There is no one method or technique that is the ONLY way to learn to read. Children learn in a variety of ways. **Read with me** is an enjoyable and uncomplicated scheme that will give your child reading confidence. Through exciting stories about Kate, Tom and Sam the dog, **Read with me**:

- *teaches the first 300 key words (75% of our everyday language) plus 500 additional words*
- *stimulates a child's language and imagination through humorous, full colour illustration*
- *introduces situations and events children can relate to*
- *encourages and develops conversation and observational skills*
- *support material includes Practice and Play Books, Flash Cards, Book and Cassette Packs*

Always praise and encourage as you go along. Keep your reading sessions short and stop immediately if your child loses interest.

Ladybird books are widely available, but in case of difficulty may be ordered by post or telephone from:

Ladybird Books – Cash Sales Department
Littlegate Road Paignton Devon TQ3 3BE
Telephone 0803 554761

A catalogue record for this book is available from the British Library

Published by Ladybird Books Ltd Loughborough Leicestershire UK
Ladybird Books Inc Auburn Maine 04210 USA

Printed in England

Read with me
The dragon den

by WILLIAM MURRAY
stories by JILL CORBY
illustrated by CHRIS RUSSELL

A shop

Here is a shop.

Tom is here.

Kate is here.

Tom is in the shop.

Kate is in the shop.

Kate likes the trees and the dragon.

Tom likes the trees
and the dragon.

Here is Sam the dog.

Sam is in the shop.

Sam the dog is here.

Sam has a toy.

No, Sam, no.

Kate has the toy.
Here is the toy.

Sam has a ball.
Sam likes the ball.

I like the ball.

Kate has a ball

and Tom has a ball.

Tom and Kate like
the trees and
the dragon.

Tom and Kate
like the dog.

Tom is in here

and Kate is in here.

Sam is in here.

Sam has the toy.
Sam likes the toy.

No,
Sam,
no.

Tom has a toy tree.

I like the toy trees.

I like Tom and Kate.

I like the dog.

No,
Sam,
no.

Here is Tom

and here is Sam.

Here is Kate.

Kate is here

and Tom is here.

Here is the dog.

Here is Sam.

Here is Tom.
Here is Kate
and here is Sam.

I like Kate and
Tom and Sam.

Words introduced in this book

Pages	*4/5*	A, shop
	6/7	Here, is, a*
	8/9	Tom, Kate, here*
	10/11	in, the
	12/13	like(s), tree(s), dragon
	14/15	Sam, dog
	16/17	has, toy
	18/19	No, no*
	20/21	ball, I
	22/23	and

Number of words used.............................19

* The same word, with or without a capital letter, is shown as it appears in the book.

All are Key Words, with the exception of Tom, Kate, Sam, dragon.

Apart from dragon, these are the same words which were introduced in Book 1 and they are all carried forward into Book 3 *The space boat*.

Sam has the toy.

No, Sam, no.

Do you remember what happened next?

LADYBIRD READING SCHEMES

Ladybird reading schemes are suitable for use with any other method of learning to read.

Say the Sounds

Ladybird's **Say the Sounds** graded reading scheme is a *phonics* scheme. It teaches children the sounds of individua letters and letter combinations, enabling them to tackle new words by building them up as a blend of smaller units.

There are 8 titles in this scheme:

1 Rocket to the jungle
2 Frog and the lollipops
3 The go-cart race
4 Pirate's treasure
5 Humpty Dumpty and the robots
6 Flying saucer
7 Dinosaur rescue
8 The accident

Support material available: Practice Books, Double Cassette Pack, Flash Cards